# EVERY LITTLE

# BAD IDEA

## CAITIE MCKAY

An imprint of Enslow Publishing

# WEST 44 BOOKS™

Please visit our website, www.west44books.com. For a free color catalog of all our high-quality books, call toll free 1-800-542-2595 or fax 1-877-542-2596.

**Cataloging-in-Publication Data**

Names: McKay, Caitie.
Title: Every little bad idea / Caitie McKay.
Description: New York : West 44, 2019. | Series: West 44 YA verse
Identifiers: ISBN 9781538382653 (pbk.) | ISBN 9781538382660 (library bound) | ISBN 9781538383339 (ebook) Subjects: LCSH: Children's poetry, American. | Children's poetry, English. | English poetry. Classification: LCC PS586.3 E947 2019 | DDC 811'.60809282--dc23

First Edition

Published in 2019 by
Enslow Publishing LLC
101 West 23rd Street, Suite #240
New York, NY 10011

Copyright © 2019 Enslow Publishing LLC

Editor: Theresa Emminizer
Designer: Sam DeMartin

Printed in the United States of America

CPSIA compliance information: Batch #CS18W44: For further information contact
Enslow Publishing LLC, New York, New York at 1-800-542-2595.

For Mom and Dad, for always being there.
And for David, for always being a really good idea.

# FRIDAY NIGHTS ARE FOR PARTIES

That's what my
best friend,
      Layla,
always says.


But Fridays are for
Mom and me.


Fridays are for
burgers and fries at Betty's.


A root beer float
passed between us.


Friday is for Betty
stopping by our table.


For Mom saying,


*Skyler Ann has been so busy.*
     *Almost done with junior year.*
       *Gonna visit colleges*
         *this summer.*

*Our college girl,*
Betty says
with a smile.


She tells us
to keep our tip,
put it toward
the college fund.

# FROM THE BEGINNING

it's always been just
        Mom and me.


Mom and me
in our two-bedroom
apartment.


Mom and me,
a small family unit.


Mom and me
against the world.


*Who needs men*
        *when we've got*
*each other?*


Mom always says.

# MY MOM, THE WARDEN

*Any results from your AP*
*science test?*
Mom asks.


*Still waiting to hear,*
I say.


*You spent a lot of time*
*on that guitar,*
Mom says.
Her lips purse.


I don't tell her that
playing Dad's old guitar
is the one time
I feel
like myself.


*I'm sure I passed,*
          I say.
*I'll try harder,*
          I promise.


Mom pats my hand,
*I know you will, baby girl.*

# NO CHOICE

but to try harder.

No choice

but to fly higher.

You see,
Grandmom had Mom
when she was only 18.

You see,
Mom only made it
to junior year
before she had me.

You see,
Mom says,
*The women in this*
*family have a*
          *w e a k n e s s*
*for bad boys.*


But not me.

No.

That could
never be.

## ONE THING FOR SURE

since the day
I was born.


Father or no father,


I'm heading to one place:
college.



Medicine.


    Law.


        Business.



Doesn't matter to Mom.


Just as long as I
make it there
and make her proud.

As long as I leave
this neighborhood—


the neon tags
I know by heart,


      the corner store
      with bars on the door,


            the brick library
            with broken windows—


for something better.

# THAT GIRL

I am that girl
who feeds your cats.

I am that girl
who waters your flowers.

I am that girl
who mows your lawn.

I am that girl
who tutors you after school.

I am that girl
who you trust
to walk your
prized poodle.

I am Skyler Wise,
that good girl
who never makes
a mistake.

I am a girl
so perfect I
fear I
might

　　　*b r e a k.*

# THE OTHER HALF

of Friday nights
is for movies.


Mom and I pop popcorn
and sit knee-to-knee
on the couch.


I pick the movie tonight,
a World War II drama,
even though Mom says
it's a bummer.


She texts on her phone
a lot…

        much more than usual.


*We can watch a different movie*
*if you hate it so much,*
I say.


Mom shakes her head.
She tries to hide
her phone behind
a pillow.

The glowing screen
gives it away.


And for the first time
I feel that
my mom is keeping
a secret.


     (There has never been
     a secret
     between us.)

# THE AWAKENING

I sit in my last English
class of junior year.


Miss Anders asks,
*Why is the final image
of* The Awakening
*so powerful?*


The room is quiet.
My classmates are on
vacation already.


I raise my hand and say,
*When Edna goes into
the water, she becomes
totally free.
Untouchable.*


Miss Anders nods.
She fixes her trendy
purple glasses
on her small pixie nose.
She's my favorite teacher
by far.

I try not to listen
as Jake Pierce says
behind my back,
*Hundred bucks to the*
*first guy to*
*finally touch*
*Skyler Wise.*

# LAYLA KEEPS A TALLY

She has made out
with 11 people.
Seven guys. Four girls.
Let five up her shirt.
Slept with two.


She keeps a tally
of her experience
the way I polish
my college application.


I have never even held
a guy's hand
and everyone at
school knows it.


Skyler Wise,
the ultimate prize.


Untouchable in every way.


That's the only way
I've been told
is safe.

# MOM ALWAYS TELLS ME

*From the very start*

*your dad*

*was a very bad*

*idea.*

# MOM'S SECRET HAS A NAME

Darron has scruffy brown hair
and a red beard.

He wears baggy jeans
and a striped sweater.

His eyes and smile are
so big I think he might be
part Muppet.

He teaches kindergarten.

He looks like one
of Santa's elves.

Some
threats
come
in
unsuspecting
packages.

# MOM WEARS A RED DRESS

I didn't even know she owned

a

red

dress.

This morning, she was my mom, wearing

those

Mom

jeans.

And now, she's some 33-year-old beauty queen wearing

a

red

dress.

# DARRON THE MUPPET

hands Mom a lily,
which is too big
for any vase we

  *o w n.*

They leave so
quickly Mom even
forgets her

  *p h o n e.*

And now I'm stuck at

  *h o m e.*

And for the first time
I feel completely

  *a l o n e.*

# SO MAYBE I HAVE ABANDONMENT ISSUES

I remember the sound
of my dad leaving.


Trees swishing.
Tires squealing.
Crunch of loose pavement
beneath his motorcycle.


He beeped twice,
same as always.


He left like he was
just getting some air


and never came back.


I have to admit,
he even looked cool
leaving me.

# THERE ARE DIFFERENT WAYS OF LEAVING

Some leave on a motorcycle

      and never come back

      and turn into postcards

      from different cities

      once a year.


Others leave in a hurry

      with a strange man

      when they promised

      it'd only ever

      be the two of you.

# THREE TIMES

*Come over.*
*Come over.*
*Come over.*

When Layla wants something,
she asks for it
three times.

She always seems to know
exactly what she wants.

*I don't know,*
I text.
*I should probably study*
*for the history exam.*

My fingers touch the cold
neck of my dad's guitar.
It's black with a
white songbird.
The strings hold a song
of a man I can
barely remember.

*That's Monday,*
Layla texts.
*That's a thousand hours away.*


*More like 70,*
I text back.


*We'll just watch a movie*
*or something,*
Layla promises.
*Like old times.*


There have been lots
of old times between us.
Making up dances
to our favorite songs.
Climbing onto
Layla's rooftop
to tell our stories
to the stars.


Old times sound good
right about now.


*Come over.*
*Come over.*
*Come over.*

# LAYLA'S FAMILY

is all I've ever wanted
in a family.

Her parents touch hands
every time they pass each other.

Her baby sister, Nova,
gives toddlers a good name.

Layla is fearless and loyal
and so completely *herself.*

And her twin brother, Zayn,
is seriously the best.

I'd say he's my second-best friend
if Layla wouldn't hate me for it.

*Getting ready for our road trip?*
Zayn asks
when I walk in the door.

Zayn has long hair,
the color of shiny chestnuts,
that hangs around
his thin shoulders.


He grows it out for
kids with cancer
and shaves it
every two years.


He's the one who taught
me how to slow dance and
make strawberry milkshakes
the *right* way.


*I can't wait*,
I say.


And I mean it.


I think I've been waiting
for this trip
my whole life.

# ZAYN AND I

are driving five hours away
at the end of the summer
to visit our
top-choice college:
Brooklea.


Zayn for robotics.
Me for pre-med.


I imagine a green campus,
lined with trees.

      I imagine brick buildings
      with white pillars.

          A library with more books
          than I've ever seen
          in one place.


Zayn gives me a thumbs-up.
I give him one back
and laugh.


*You dorks*, Layla says,
as she walks in the room.

# LAYLA LIED

The hair straightener is hot.
The eye shadow kit is out.
Nail polishes are lined up
in a neat rainbow row.


*You said we were staying in*,
I say.


Layla puts her hands
on her hips.


*It's Friday night, girlie.*
*It's time to party.*
She dances around
in her slippers.


But
I don't party.


Especially at
the complex.

# THE COMPLEX

is a group of
apartment buildings
on the edge of our neighborhood,
near Riggins Creek.
Apartments hosting parties
have rubber bands on
the doorknobs.
Parties at the complex
are where most Monday morning
stories come from.


Layla asks,
*What's holding you back?*


*Nothing is holding me—*


*Wise One, come on,*
Layla says.
*Even your mom is out tonight.*


Layla calls me Wise One
because that's what my
T-ball shirt said
when we met.
We were seven.

*Which is a bad idea,*
I point out.


*And so what?*
Layla says.


*Sometimes it's a*
*good idea*
*to act on a*
*bad idea.*

# I'M ABOUT TO ARGUE

but I think about Mom's
red dress,
the smile on her lips
as she left the door.


If Mom can break
her promise to me,
then I can break
my promise to her.


And that's how I end up
letting Layla give me a
makeover.


That's how I end up
in a short black skirt
and a too-small top
that shows my shoulders.


That's how I
end up acting on
my first
very bad idea.

# THE THREE BEARS

We walk into three parties
before finding the
right one.


The first had a too-old crowd.


The second had a too-stoned crowd.


The third had some familiar faces
and a whole keg.


Like the story of the three bears,
this one was just right.


At least according to Layla.

# OPEN SEASON

Layla gives hugs like
free candy.

I cross my arms
and try to stay small.

A few people say hi,
raise their eyebrows when
they see me there.

Jake Pierce puts his
arm around me
and announces,
*Open season, y'all.*

I shrug away.

The music pounds.
People yell.

*Going outside for air*,
I say to Layla.

But she can't hear.

So I walk out
the back door
and try to

*d i s a p p e a r.*

# AND THAT'S WHEN

I see a boy,
with jeans ripped at the knees.

> With a black T-shirt
> and raven-black hair.

> > With blue eyes so sharp
> > they seem to have
> > edges.

# HE SITS ON A LEDGE

that separates the complex
from the creek.


Not part of any party.


He watches us,
like some kind of god.


He nods his head
       at someone.


Wait.


At me.


I walk over,
and he holds out a hand
to help me up.

# TRADING NAMES

He asks my name.


I pause.


*I hate my name*,
I say.


My dad wanted me to be Tyler,
after some last name
of some singer
in some '80s band.


When I was born a girl,
he called me Skyler instead.
Filled out the papers
while Mom was
drugged and sleeping.


My mom hates my name too.
She calls me Skyla-Ann, real quick.
So fast it doesn't feel
connected to me.

The boy looks at me
with those deep-blue eyes
until I tell him.


*I'll call you Sky,*

he says.

*Because you look like the*

*kind of girl*

*who shouldn't*

*be tied*

*to the*

*ground.*

# HIS NAME IS COLE BAKER

He goes to PS 17.
A senior.
He lives at the complex.


*Complex parties are for losers.*
*It's good you left.*


*Have you ever been to one?*
I ask.


Cole laughs.
*Of course.*
*When I was a kid.*
*I can show you a real party*
*if you like.*


His words make me shiver.
They go down smooth
like ice cream
on a scratchy throat.


When I don't answer,
he asks,
*What do you want*
*out of life, Sky?*

*I'm going to college
after next year,*
I say.


Cole hmms.
*College for what?*


*Pre-med,*
I say.


*Practical,*
he says.
*Now, what do you
really want?*

# I JUST STARE

because

I thought I knew.

Because

I thought that answer
      was so clear.

Because

I don't know.

No one

      has ever asked
      me that before.

# COLE JUMPS OFF THE LEDGE

*Jump.*

*I'll catch you,*

       he promises.

So against

       my better judgment

I leave the ledge

       and let myself

          f

          a

          l

          l

# MAGNETISM

I text Layla,
*I'm walking home.*
*Be safe.*


She won't mind that
I'm gone.
I was probably just
her social charity case
tonight.


Cole is so tall,
his shoulders so wide,
I feel like I have
my own personal
bodyguard.


We don't talk
as we walk
down the chalk-
covered streets
to my apartment.


I feel a magnetic field
dancing between
our hands.

No one has ever
held my hand.

Safest that way.

(Bad idea, Sky.)

Our wrists bump,
knuckles brush.

Then our fingers
slide into the spaces
between.

Spaces I never knew
were empty.

*You're shaking,*
he says.

*It's cold,*
I say, even though
the air is warm
with the start of summer.

# WHEN I GET HOME

the lights are out.
The house is dark
and empty.


Cole's eyes ask
if he can come up.


I say,
*I better get in.*


He nods like he understands.
What a gentleman.
Maybe he's not a bad boy
like Mom warned me about—
even with his
ripped jeans.


Cole takes my phone
from my hand,
puts his number in.


He touches my chin,
leans in like he might
kiss me.

*Text me,*
he whispers.


Then he smirks
and turns.
Walks away.


My.
Heart.
Is.
Pounding.

# I EXPECT

Mom to get home
before 10.
She likes to get
eight hours of sleep
before Saturday shifts
at the factory.


She gets home at midnight.


I sit on the couch,
textbook on my knees.


I expect
Mom to ask
about my night.


I expect
myself to
have a hard time
lying.


But she doesn't ask
and I don't tell.

We both smile
and go
our separate ways.


Now that
I did not
expect.

# WHERE DID YOU GO?

Layla texts me.


I get the text at
four in the morning.


How can I explain
how it feels
when someone suddenly
plugs you in?


When electricity
          races
through your veins
          for the first time
and you're suddenly


              *on.*


Suddenly you're
          someone new.


*Meet me tomorrow at Betty's,*
          I text back.
*I'll tell you everything.*

# STOP STARING

Layla says,
dumping syrup
on her pancake.
*I know I look
like death.*

I laugh at her
and she looks up.
She knows something
is different.

Everything feels different.

*I met someone,*
I say.

Her eyebrows rise.
She's suddenly awake.

*Who?*
She nearly screams.

*His name is Cole,*
I say.
*Cole Baker.*

I like the way
his name sounds
like heat.


Layla's eyes go wide.
*Cole Baker?*
*Tall kid, black hair?*


*You know him?*
I ask,
hopeful.


*Know him?*
Layla asks.
*He's a legend.*


She shakes her head.


*And he's not good*
        *for you.*

# WHAT KIND OF A LEGEND?

There are heroes in
legends, knights
who save girls
from near death.

I can see Cole like that.
He seems like the
guy who swoops in
to save the day.

*Not the good kind*,
Layla says.
She picks at her
pancake with a fork.
*Let's just say,*
*he's done it all.*

*He holds the record*
*for number of beers*
*in one night*
*at a complex party.*

*He got busted last*
*year for selling pills*
*in school.*

*He hangs out with
a bad crowd.*

*Oh,
and last year.*

Layla's voice goes low.

*He stole a car
and crashed it
into the creek.
Passenger was hurt,
like…almost died.
Cole was sent to juvie,
but word is,
he ran away.*

I shake my head.
*It can't be the same guy.*

I think of his fingers
between mine,
strong but soft.

*Oh, it's the same guy,*
Layla says.
*Be smart,
Wise One.*

# A DAY FULL OF FIRSTS

Layla has never
told me to be smart.

It gives me a tiny
jolt, thinking that
she's worried about me.

No one ever worries
          about me.

Everyone knows
I will always
do
the
right
thing.

# QUESTIONS

*What do you want out of life, Sky?*

I can hear Cole's voice
in my head.

Do I want to sit home studying
      all day
      all night
      until college?

Do I want to play guitar
      to an
      empty room
      until college?

Do I want to be Skyler Wise
      the untouched,
      the ultimate prize
      until college?

Everything I thought
I knew for sure
now ends with a
      question mark.

# SUMMER IS WAITING

I'm pretty sure
I aced my history exam.
Even if my brain
was clouded by Cole.

Every time I tried to
focus, I saw those
sharp-blue eyes.

Now summer is waiting
outside my window.
And I sit inside,
weighing my options.
What kind of summer
do I want?

Mom calls from
the kitchen.
She's leaving with
Darron.

I wait until I'm alone
and then I pick up
          my phone
and text him.


(What's the worst
that can happen?)

# COLE IS HERE WITHIN THE HOUR

(I am not sure
      I've breathed
            this whole hour.)


He gets out of his black Grand Am
to let me in.


(His hand on my back
      sends a shock
            down my spine.)


We drive out of the neighborhood.


(Goodbye, neon tags.
      Goodbye, corner store.
            Goodbye, broken library.)


We drive to the city.


(Radio turned up so loud
      the bumping bass
            replaces my heartbeat.)

# BURNING BRIDGES

Cole puts the car in park
at the foot of a bridge.

*This city is full
of bridges,*
I say,
to make small talk.

*More to burn,*
he says.

When he smiles,
there's fire in his eyes.

He takes my hand
       (electric shock)
and leads me over the bridge.

It's dark now,
hard to see where I'm walking.

*Step over,*
he says.

I follow him over
a barrier
and then realize
I am only an inch
from falling
into the river.


I start to climb back
to safety,
but Cole holds me
tight around the waist.
I couldn't wriggle away
if I tried.


I close my eyes
and hope gravity
is on my side.


*Shh,*
he says.
*It's okay.*
*I've got you.*
*Open your eyes.*


So I do.

And I swear,
every light in the city—

       yellow

       pink

       blue

       white—

is on for us
in that moment
as we stand
on the edge.


I've never felt so scared.


(I've never felt so alive.)

## LIKE CINDERELLA

Cole gets me home
at midnight.


My curfew was two hours ago
and I have five texts
from Mom.


I've *never* ignored
a text from Mom.


But somehow this
was worth it.


At one point,
Cole pulled my hair
out of its tight
ponytail.


*You look beautiful*
*when you let loose,*
he said,
placing a finger under
my chin.

That's the first time
anyone has called me
beautiful, with my plain
brown hair and plain
brown eyes.


I looked in a store window
as he bought me tacos
and realized I looked
like a whole new person.


Not Skyler Wise.
Wise One.
Skyla-Ann.


*Sky.*


Untethered
      like a bird,
      like a hot-air balloon,
      like a dragonfly
beating its wings
to fly so high.


I walk inside and see
Mom's eyes are red
and puffy.


*Where have you been?*

# I AM FROZEN

I have

never

      ever

            ever

made my mom cry.


*I'm so sorry, Mom.*


She shakes her head.
*If you're staying late*
*at Layla's*
*you need to let me know.*


She probably thinks
Layla, Zayn, and I
were watching a movie.


She doesn't have a clue
about the bridge,
about the lights,
about the city,
about my heart.

And I know I could
never tell her. Ever.


*I won't do it again,*
I say.


I try to tell myself
it's not a lie
to keep a
burning truth
locked inside.

# TINY BREAKABLE THINGS

It's my first summer shift
at St. Blaze's Hospital.

I worked here last year—
folding linens and
stocking supplies—
that kind of thing.

Volunteering looks good
on a college application.

But it's more than that.

I love being in a place
that fixes people,
that saves people,
that sees people
through life and death.

Everything makes sense here.

Today, the head nurse,
Stacy,
asks me to do a bigger job.

My new job is to hold
the babies
who are too tiny and weak
to take home.


*Some are addicted
from the moment
they're born,*
Stacy says.


*They cry and cry.
They need someone calm
and dependable.
They need someone like you.*


*Now you're not 18, but...
we can make an
exception
for an exceptional
person.*

# NICU

Stacy takes me to the NICU.
She has me sit in a rocking chair.
She hands me the
smallest baby
I have ever seen.


Her eyelids are see-through-
almost-blue.

Her skin is as pink and thin
as tissue paper.

She's so light,
it feels more like holding
a kitten than a human.


She fusses and cries
for a moment,
but settles in.


*I knew you were the right one*
*for this job,*
Stacy says.
She smiles and
squeezes my shoulder.

All I know
is that I've read science books,
aced biology tests,
and looked at cells under
a microscope.


But I've never felt more
sure about being a
doctor.


I've never felt more
sure about taking tiny
breakable things
and saving them.

# LONG DAY

I come home and throw myself
on the couch.

*Long day, baby girl?*
Mom asks.

I cuddled eight babies,
folded linens,
and helped a screaming
patient back to her
bed.
*You have no idea*,
I say with a laugh.

But she *does* know—
Mom works more
than anyone.

Mom is dressed for
her second job.

She works most days at a
factory making lip balms
and nights cashing
at a CVS.

*Well, you can order whatever movie
you want tonight
on the TV,*
she says.
*I'll foot the bill.*


I smile, and start to say
thank you
but my phone buzzes.


It's him.


I must jump 10 feet
off the couch.


*It's Layla!*
I lie.


(Again.)


(How is it so easy?)


*Looks like someone
got her energy back,*
Mom says
with a laugh.

# COLE PICKS ME UP

This time, he doesn't
open the car door.


He just waves from inside.


I get in and smell smoke.
Why didn't I smell it the
other night?


*Do you smoke?*
I ask.
He takes a cigarette from
his pocket and offers
me one.


*No thanks,*
I say.
I start to wonder if this
is a bad idea.


*Where do you want to go, Sky?*
Cole asks,
as he reverses the car
and then speeds
onto the road.

*I don't know,*
I say.
*Surprise me.*

# WE DRIVE SO FAR

that I start to think he's kidnapped me.
What if Layla's stories were true?

(They can't be.)

We talk about music.
He knows all the bands
in my dad's collection.
The CDs he left behind.


He knows everything from
Tracy Chapman to
the Beatles to
Tupac,
can recite the lyrics
off the top of his head.


We talk about me.


He thinks it's so funny
that I don't swear.

       He thinks it's so cute
       that I'm friends with my mom.

           He thinks it's so weird
           that I alphabetize my books.

It's like he's doing a case study
    in *me*.


He's looking closer
than anyone ever has.

# THE AIR HERE

smells fishy and damp.
The sky is purple-red.


The water is dark and angry.
White caps crash against the shore.


I take off my shoes to walk
on the cold, fine sand.


*I haven't been to the beach*
*since I was a kid,*
I say.
*My dad used to bring me.*


*Why'd he stop?*
Cole asks.


*He left when I was five,*
I say.
*On a motorcycle.*


I pause.

*You don't have a motorcycle…*
*do you?*


Cole shakes his head.
*I don't.*


He pauses.


*And anyone would be a fool*
*to leave you.*


Cole stands behind me
and wraps his arms around
my chest, holding
every bit of me in.


I feel his lips on
the back of my head.


And it feels like home.

# CARRIED AWAY

It starts to rain.
What a way
to ruin a day
at the beach.


But Cole runs out
into the water,
the crashing surf.


I follow him
and stand at the edge.
*I can't swim*,
I say.


He comes over,
picks me up,
and carries me in.


The water pushes and pulls
on my body,
but for the first time
in my life
I don't mind
getting
      carried
          away.

# HERE ARE THE THINGS I LEARN ABOUT COLE BAKER

1. He has a dog named Hendrix that he loves more than life.

2. He doesn't have a father either.

3. His mother isn't home much.

4. He knows how to make lasagna from scratch.

5. He visits his grandma once a week to bring her cigarettes and magazines.

6. He can put a car together from scrap.

7. He was a Cub Scout until he was 10.

# THE PINK ON HIS FACE

seems to deepen
with each thing
he admits.

The more Cole and I talk,
the more I know
he is not the boy
other people think
he is.

He's more than cigarettes,
numbered beers,
and stolen cars.

I look into his blue eyes
and know he's got
a heart as wide
as the ocean.

The last thing I learn about Cole that night:

He's got a kiss
that makes me
     *f o r g e t*
everything I once
thought was
true.

# GOOD KIDS AND BAD KIDS

Cole drops me off
at my apartment building.

Mom isn't home—
perfect.

I want to tell her
          everything,
but I know that's
not possible.

Cole pulls away
in his car.

Just then,
I see Miss Anders,
my English teacher.
She lives in the
apartment building
across the street.

She crosses the street
and says,
*Are you seeing
Cole Baker?*

My heart swells
to my face.
All of me
turns red at once.


*Yes,*
I say,
my chin up.
*I guess I am.*


Miss Anders shakes
her head.
*You're just such*
*a good kid.*
*And he's just…*
            *not.*


I always thought
Miss Anders was
the cool teacher.
She's young, smart,
and even swears sometimes.


But now, I think
it's me and Cole
against Miss Anders.

Me and Cole against
the world.

No one understands.

No one sees the real him.

No one knows him

better than me.

# MOM'S SMILE

is like the first tree
to bloom white and pink
flowers in spring.


You never know
when to expect it.


You never know
how long it'll last.


And you have never seen
something so quick
and so beautiful.


Mom has a space
between her front
teeth.


She has big lips
that don't need lipstick
and a dimple
in her right cheek.

Since Darron came around
it's like the first day
of spring every day.


I wonder
why so many of our days
were winter
when it was just


      Mom and me.

# HOW ARE YOU DOING, BABY GIRL?

Mom is chopping garlic
for red sauce,
humming a happy song.


*Great*,
I say, a little
breathless.
Cole is texting me
pure poetry
about bridges
and sunsets
and us.


*I'm sorry I haven't
been around lately*,
Mom says.


She pauses.


*Do you like Darron?*


I pause.


Then nod.

*He's...nice.*

(He's nice but I wonder
why he's even around.
We never needed him before.)

Mom sets the knife down.
*He is…isn't he?*
*God, it's so good*
*to be with a good man*
*for once.*

(Good men don't all
have to look like Muppets
and teach kindergarten.)

Cole texts and asks me
if I can go with him
on an adventure.

*Layla needs me,*
I say.
*Bad breakup.*

*It's spaghetti night,*
Mom says, frowning.
*That's always*
*our special dinner.*

*More for you and Darron,*
I say.

(You won't even notice
that I'm gone.)

Mom kisses me
on the cheek
and I go.

# TIME

Time flies
in summertime
when the sun is high
and ice cream melts
down your fingers.


Time flies
when nights hug you
like a warm blanket
and stars fight their way
through city lights.


Time flies
when arms wrap around
your waist and lips
taste like blue slushies
and sunlight.


Time flies
when every sunset
is pink and purple
and every song
on the radio was
written for you.

Time flies
when you are

f

a

l

l

i

n

g

in love.

# MY ROOM

has always been
my own private space.


The mint-green walls.
A calendar full of quotes
from famous scientists.
My dry-erase board
with a packed-tight schedule.
My bedspread with
dragonflies that Mom
bought me last birthday.


But now, my room
feels different.
Because Cole is here
and Mom is not.


She's out on a date
and I'm in on a date.


Cole sits on my bed
and points to Dad's guitar.
*You play?* he asks.

*Kind of,* I say.
*No lessons or anything.*
*Just video classes online.*


I don't say that
playing guitar is
my way of talking
to my dad.


*Play for me,*
Cole says.


No one has ever
asked me to play.
Mom tells me I
could be doing
something else.
Layla makes a joke
about me being
Miss Rock Star.


*Please?*
Cole asks.

# SO I PLAY FOR HIM

My fingers
        dance
along the
        silver strings.

A song
        my dad
once played
        for me.

A song about secret chords
        and victory marches
and kitchen chairs
        and marble arches.

And Cole
        listens to
every note,
        his eyes on me.

Someone
finally
hears me.
*Hallelujah*.

# THE PLAYGROUND

Mom used to tell me
to leave the playground
when the streetlights
come on.

Now, I wait until
the streetlights are on
and Mom is asleep
to make my escape.

Cole and I sit on the
sagging bridge
between the slide
and the monkey bars.

We do this every night,
kissing and talking
in a blanket of darkness.
Our safe space.

I lay my head
on his chest and
listen to his strong
beating heart.

And then comes the
night when he says
*I love you* and I become
just another puddle
on the playground.

# LAYLA LOVES EVERYONE

That's why I'm surprised
when she hates Cole.


Cole buys us pizza
and we eat outside
under a blue umbrella.


Layla eyes Cole up
and down
and up
and down.


Cole mostly looks
at his food.
He gives
one-word answers.


*He's a jerk,*
Layla says later.
*I can just tell.*


*She seems stuck up,*
Cole says later,
with a shrug.

Why can't the two people
I'm closest to
just get along?


That night,
Layla texts me
and says she's
                worried
about me.


I don't respond.

# PERFECT LITTLE BUBBLE

It's been five weeks.

Five amazing weeks.

*Why haven't I
met your friends yet?*
I ask Cole.

He's tracing
hearts on my palm.

*You wouldn't like them,*
he says and shrugs.

*Well, I like you,*
I say.
*And you like them.*

Cole pulls his hand away.
I flinch.

Sometimes he reacts
too quickly.

*They won't like me,*
*you mean,*
I say.


I don't tell him my fear.
That he will leave me
if I don't fit in
with the rest
of his life.


Opposites may
            attract,
but birds of different feathers
            must find a common nest.


We've been in such
a perfect little bubble
but the edges
feel as if
they might wear
thin.


*What can I do*
*to make them like me?*

# PEACE OFFERING

Cole suggests
I bring a case
of beer.


*I can't buy beer,*
I say.
*I'm 16.*


*With a face like that*
*and a body like that,*
*you could buy*
*whatever you want,*
Cole says,
with that smile
and those eyes.


He traces his finger
from my face
to my waist
until I have
to laugh.


Being with Cole
makes me want to
jump even when I'm
scared.

He seems so sure
there will be a
safe landing.

He makes
every
little
bad
idea
seem like a
good one.


*Okay*,
I say,
surprising myself.


*I'll do it.*

# FRIENDS IN LOW PLACES

Cole's friends
are unlike anyone I've
ever met.

He warns me
before I meet them.

He warns them
before they meet me.

One has teeth missing.
One has a black eye.
One has tattoos on his fingers.
One has huge holes in his earlobes.
One is just super, super stoned.

I feel five sets
of eyes on me.

I hand out five beers.

I get five crooked grins.

*Aren't you gonna have one?*
Missing Teeth asks.


*Um.*


Cole opens one and
puts it in my hand.


*Yeah, she will,*
he says.


I take my first sip
of beer, and it
fizzes down
my throat.


Bitter on my tongue.


I watch the clock
as they drink and
smoke,
and wait until


Cole is mine again.

## HERE'S A THING NO ONE KNOWS ABOUT COLE BAKER

He

cries.

Just like a

baby in the NICU or

my mom at the end of a good

movie. Just like me, when my dad

stopped coming home. I walk Cole home

as he swerves and stumbles. He's had too much

to drink. I want to be mad. But then he stops. He takes

both of my hands. He looks at me hard with those blue eyes.

And then he starts to cry. He says he loves me. He says,

*Don't leave me.* He says I have changed his life.

And he could never live without me.

# RUN AWAY

Cole is quiet
as he tiptoes across
our apartment
and into my room.


I'm not sure how
Mom doesn't hear
him. She would
totally freak out.


Cole's mom kicked
him out again.
He argued with
her druggy boyfriend.


I lock my door.
He sits on my pink
rug and pulls me
onto his lap.


*I wish we could
just run away,*
he says.

*To a place where*
*no one can find us.*


    *Think of it,*
    he says.
    *Our own apartment,*
    *just the two of us*
    *together.*


    *I'll get a job,*
    he says.
    *And you can*
    *write songs and*
    *raise the kids.*


*I'll marry you,*
he says.
*Right now.*
*I swear.*


I consider this
new kind of home,
us together,
a future
I never planned.

# COLLEGE FIRST

I insist.


(I sound like
my mom.)


*You know I'll*
*find a way*
*to keep you here*,
he says.


He tickles me until
I laugh out of
habit.


I can't tell if
it's his words
or his fingers
that send a shiver
down
my
spine.

# 9 A.M. IS EARLY

when you sneak out
late to kiss
and play guitar
by the creek.

9 a.m. is early

when you spend
the last hours of night
jumping from
the Riggins Creek bridge,
shrieking into the
dark.

9 a.m. is early

when you spend
sunrise in the arms
of the one you love,
hearts beating in time.

9 a.m. is early

and I am late.

# THE HOSPITAL

looks different
when I know I've
broken the rules.


I slept through
four alarms,
and now I'm
*late*
*late*
*late.*


Nurse Stacy
holds a baby
in the NICU.


When she sees me,
she frowns.


*I had other things*
*to do today, you know,*
Stacy says.
*Now I'm late with*
*my rounds.*

*I'm so sorry,*
I say.


I brush my shower-wet hair
out of my face
and sit down.


I offer my arms
for her to set
the baby in.


She sets the baby
in my arms
and it starts
to cry.


*The baby can tell*
*how you're feeling,*
Stacy says.
*These babies need you to be*
*strong and dependable*
*and calm.*


I take a deep breath.
I think of something calm,
of Mom and me
watching a movie
like we used to.

(So many Fridays ago.)


The baby stops crying.
Stacy's face softens.
*See?*
*She*
*recognizes*
*you.*


For some reason
that makes me want
to cry.


(I wonder for a moment
if
I
recognize
myself.)

# SO HIGH

Cole has a surprise for me.
*Bring your guitar*, he says.


He drives me to the city.
A little cafe called *Six Feet Under*.


The cafe smells like toast and coffee.
It has Day of the Dead skull decorations.


Cole carries my guitar.
He says, *I got you a spot.*


*I can't*, I say. *I can't just play
in front of people.*


Cole hands me my guitar.
He nods to the stage.


*The whole world needs
to hear your voice, Sky.*


When my name is called,
I let my feet take me to the stage.

I clear my throat, set my fingers.
They shake against the strings.


I look at Cole and his eyes
are locked on me. I breathe.


I start to sing and people listen.
My voice fills the whole room.


My voice may shake, but it is there.
It is bright and real and mine.


When the song ends, I am
high. So, so high.

# I HAVE TO GO

That's how
          most
of our nights end.


He says my mom
          controls
my every move.


He says I should be
          free
to do what I want.


He just doesn't get
          why
I need to go home.


Probably because he has no
          home
to go home to.

# COLE IS PERFECT BUT

sometimes he
forgets
to
call.

Sometimes he
calls
me
stupid.

Sometimes he
pulls
away
quickly.

Sometimes he
drinks
all
day.

Sometimes he
lies
about
it.


But that's only
some of the time.

# OUT OF PLACE

I bring Cole to
Layla's house.
Her family has a party
every summer.
The whole neighborhood
is invited. A potluck feast.
Mom is out with Darron,
and almost never talks to
neighborhood people,
so my secret is safe.
There are drinks, food,
and fireworks.


It's my favorite summer event.


But Cole is in a mood.
He won't hold my hand.
He sulks by the driveway
smoking a cigarette,
even though he quit
last week.


This is not going so well.

I load my plate
with tamales and rice
and roti and lentils.
Then I feel a light
tug on my ponytail.
Zayn has done that
since we were kids.
*Hey, Wise One,*
he says.
*Just two weeks until Brooklea!*


Cole is watching us with hawk eyes.


*Can't wait!*
I say and smile.
Cole comes over,
takes my hand,
and stares Zayn down
until Zayn says, *Sorry?*
and backs away.


Cole wants to know what we were talking about.


*Nothing*, I say.
*Just our road trip.*
And then I remember
that I've never told Cole
about the road trip.

And this makes Cole really mad.

*You're going*
*on a trip*
*with that guy?*
he says
through his teeth.
*When you've never even*
*spent the night with me?*

He's never been this angry with me.

*I'm going to visit*
*a college*, I say.
*I told you*
*it was always my dream*
*to go.*

I touch his arm. Try to bring him back.

*You think you're*
*better than me,*
*don't you?*
Cole says.
*Wake up, Sky,*
*no one from here*
*goes to college.*
*Wake up, Sky,*
*you can't have that*
*and me both.*

# *I LOVE YOU* IS A BAND-AID

We make up.

We always do.

We kiss.

And cry.

And say *I love you*.

And promise

to never leave

one another.

And things

are okay

just for

a moment.

# THERE'S NO BAND-AID FOR FRIENDSHIP

**Layla texts:**
*You left the party
early. You left
before the fireworks.*

        **I text:**
        *I'm sorry. Cole and I
        needed to talk. Things are
        better now though.*

**She texts:**
*That party is our favorite
summer tradition
and you left it.*

        **I text:**
        *I thought you'd
        understand.*

**She texts:**
*I hope he really
makes you happy.
I hope he's really
worth it.*

**I text:**
*He is, Layla.*
*He really is.*


And that's the last time
　　　we text each other.

# OVER TIME

Cole's eyes

> turn from sharp blue
> to steel-gray.

Cole's hands

> turn from soft and gentle
> to rough and wanting.

Cole's words

> turn from poetry
> to biting comments.

Cole's lips

> no longer feel
> like a safe harbor.

Cole changes

> little by little
> day by day.

And I don't know

> what I can do
> to stop it.

# MY MOM, THE DRILL SERGEANT

*What do you say*
*when a boy tries*
*to force you*
*to do something you're*
*not ready to do?*

Mom used to ask
when I was a kid.

> *NO!*
> I'd shout.

*What do you say*
*when someone*
*pushes the limits*
*you make?*

> *NO!*
> I'd shout.

*What do you say*
*when someone tries*
*to make you stray*
*from your path?*

> *NO!*
> I'd shout.

*Good girl,*
she'd say.

# GOOD GIRL BUT

it's hard to resist
after a long kiss
and *I love yous.*


It's hard to resist
when he says
all the right things.


It's hard to resist
when *nos* turn to *maybes*
and *maybes* turn to *soon.*


And that *soon*
reminds me of time
and how it is still moving.


I look at the clock
on Cole's dashboard
and know that *soon*
will not be *soon enough*
to get home.


It's 1 a.m. and
I am so dead.

# I TELL A GOOD STORY

That's what Miss Anders
said last year when I
took her creative writing
class.


*You know just when
to use the right
character.*


*You know just when
to hold back from
telling it all.*


*You know just when
to add little details
to keep it real.*


Miss Anders may be right.
But she never told me how
to keep a story going
when the web catches
a snag and breaks.

# I TOLD MOM

I was going to Layla's
but she called Layla's
and I was not there.


Mom is on the couch
when I arrive
well after 2 a.m.


*Layla told me*
*about your boyfriend,*
Mom says.
Her eyes are torches.


*Mom—*


Mom twists a blanket
in her hands,
tighter and tighter.
*She told me*
*you've been*
*seeing him*
*all summer.*


*Mom,*
I say.
*I can explain.*

# I CAN EXPLAIN BUT

Mom doesn't
      let me
explain.


Mom doesn't
      listen
to all the
      good things
about Cole.


Mom doesn't
      care
what's in my
      heart.


She points a
      finger
at me and says,
      *Listen,*
*we agreed no*
      *dating*
*until you get to*
      *college.*

# I BOIL OVER

*Just because you*
*made a mistake*
*doesn't mean*
*I don't get*
*to live my life,*
I say.


(My words
are fast
and fake.)


*You never listen*
*to what I want.*


(My voice
doesn't even
sound like mine.)


*You don't know*
          *anything*
*about my mistakes,*
Mom says.

*Or else you*
*wouldn't be*
*seeing that boy*
*and keeping secrets.*

*I had to keep him*
*a secret, Mom,*
I say.
*You wouldn't*
*have kept an*
*open mind.*


She says,
*There are no*
*secrets between us.*


*Lying is a*
*bad idea, Skyla-Ann.*

# I WOULD GIVE ANYTHING

to have Mom
look at me
the way she
did before tonight.


Mom shakes her head.


*I can't tell if*
*I failed you*
*as a mother.*
*Or you*
*failed me*
*as a daughter.*

# GROUNDED

Two weeks.

No laptop.

No cell phone.

No TV.

No guitar.

No Cole.

# IN BETWEEN

The one thing I have
is the hospital.
It is clean and white
and the baby room
is full of pink
and blue blankets.


Here, I can hold
onto something
more fragile
than my heart
and rock it until
it calms down.


Here, I'm someone
who is not Perfect Skyler Ann
   for Mom
and not Rebel Sky
   for Cole
but something
separate and
in between.

# COLE CATCHES ME

outside of the
emergency room.


*Finally*, he says.
He pulls me in close,
hugs me like it's
been years.


God, I missed
the way he smells
like cinnamon gum,
gasoline,
and campfire.


*Finally*, I say.
I hold my breath.
I know our stolen
moment will end
as soon as I
let it go.

# COME WITH ME

*Come with me,*
      *where we can be*
*all alone and spend*
      *the night in*
*each other's arms,*
      Cole says.


Cole is not like
      Layla.
He will only ask
      once.

# A CABIN

in the woods,
the one thing
Cole's dad
gives him,
one weekend
a year.

A hunting cabin
an hour away,
farther than
I've ever been.
Overnight.

A cabin.
Far away.
Overnight.
With a boy.

It will be
the biggest lie
I've ever told.
The biggest
secret between
Mom and I.

## THERE'S NO WAY

That's what I tell Cole.
I'll
      still
           be
                 grounded.

But he says that if
I
      really
           love
                 him,

I will try
to
      find
           a
                 way.


And if not, then he's not sure
if
      he
           can
                 wait.

# A ROCK AND A HARD PLACE

I have a choice to make.

> Go with Cole
> next weekend
> and lose my Mom's
> trust.

Or.

> Stay home
> and lose Cole
> forever.

I have a choice to make.

> Say yes to Cole,
> give him everything
> so we can be okay.

Or.

> Say no to Cole
> and watch him

> slowly
>                 slip
>                         *a w a y.*

# THERE'S JUST ONE PROBLEM

Something I totally forgot.


That weekend.
          *The* weekend.
When I am going to
          lose it
in a cabin
          in the woods.


Yeah, see,
          it's that weekend
when Zayn and I
          planned to go
on our road trip
          to Brooklea.


The one place
          I've always
wanted to go.


The one goal
          I've always
held close
                    to
                    my
                    heart.

# PASS THE BUTTER

That's how I know
Mom has forgiven me.


We sit at the table,
just the two of us.
Spaghetti night.


*Mom*, I say,
my voice trembling.
*Can I still go
to Brooklea?*


She says she'll
have to think
about it.


But we both know
that she will say
yes and let me go.


College is the one
thing that has always
been a *yes* in this home.

# THE FUNNY THING ABOUT LOVE

is

how

it

takes

you

over

so

completely

that

you

lose

yourself

piece

by

piece.

# COLE DRIVES BY

that night, same as
he has done for the
past two weeks.

He looks up at my
window and I hold up
my dry-erase board.

It used to have my
classes and activities on it
so I could stay on track.

But tonight
it does not say *no*,
it does not say *maybe*,
it does not say *soon*.

For the first time
I give him the
three letters he's
always wanted.

Y
E
S

# THE FIRST CALL

Zayn.
I call him Friday morning.
Just hours before
I will leave with Cole.


*I'm so sorry,*
I say, making my voice
scratchy.
*It must be a summer cold.*
*I can't get out of bed.*


Zayn pauses.
I nearly break.


He knows me better
than anyone besides
Layla and Mom.


We spent countless
Sunday mornings together
after sleepovers.
Before Layla woke up.

He made me
apple pancakes
and put on old
'80s movies.

He taught me
how to dance the
moonwalk.

He stayed up with me
when I missed my mom
and couldn't sleep.

*Are you sure?*
Zayn asks.
*This is all
you've ever
wanted, Skyler.*

I swear it's the
first time
I've heard my real name
in weeks.

Not Sky.
Skyler.

My throat is tight.
*Yeah,*
I say.
*Go without me.*

# I CALL LAYLA

before Zayn
can break the news
to her.


I tell her how I need her.


She says,
*You haven't needed me
all summer.*


I tell her how
I need her to lie
to my mom.


*Are you listening to yourself?*
she asks,
and I feel shame
deep in my bones.


I make my voice tough
like hers.
*Don't pretend you're
perfect, Lay.
How many people
are on your list?*

She hangs up on me.


I know she'll
lie for me, even
if she hates me right now.


That's what best friends do.

# SHE AND ME

Mom and Darron sit

      on the couch

      knee-to-knee.

Just how *we*

      used to be.

And I see

      how we

      may never be

      just we

ever again.

# SECOND LIES

roll more easily
toward the tip
of the tongue.


Like a bowling ball
toward pins,
following a
well-worn path.


*Heading out to Layla's,*
I say.


Even though
I haven't
been there
in weeks.


    Even though
    she might
    hate my guts.


        Even though
        I haven't even
        told her
        what I'm about
        to do.

*We're leaving for our trip*
*first thing*
*in the morning,*
I lie.


Mom stands up,
looks at me a
long moment.


I wonder if
she can see
the lies
like tattoos
on my skin.

# BUT INSTEAD

Mom folds me
in her arms.

She smells my hair
the way she always
does. The way I smell
the sweet heads
of the babies in
the hospital.

I wonder if I will
smell the same,
after my *yes*.

My stomach feels
full of moths
trying to get out
toward the light.

*I love you, Mom,*
I say.
My voice shakes.

*I am so, so proud,*
Mom says,
hands on my shoulders.
*My college girl.*


She has tears in her eyes.
She has put her trust in me
again and I don't deserve it.


I pull away,
fake a smile.
*I better go,*
I say.


Almost hoping
she'll beg
me to

*s t a y.*

# INTO THE SUNSET

I recognize the sound
of Cole arriving.

Trees swishing.
Tires squealing.
Crunch of loose pavement
beneath his Grand Am.

Cole picks me up
a mile from my house
just as the streetlights
flicker on.

I slide into the
seat. Our getaway car.

I slide my fingers
into his
and it feels warm
and safe.

I feel so felt.

I wonder if this
is that moment
I've always waited for.

The one from
all my storybooks.

The one my mom
told me I deserved.

The one when
my prince and I
ride off
into the sunset.

# I COUNT MINUTES

**8:47:**
Cole tells me
how happy he is
I decided to come
with him.

**8:48:**
I open the window
and try to catch
a full breath.

**8:49:**
Cole says we are
almost there.
He squeezes
my thigh.

**8:50:**
I think I'm
going to be sick.

**8:51:**
We arrive at
the cabin.
My legs move
me forward.

**8:52:**
We are inside.
This might be
a really bad idea.

**8:53:**
*All alone,*
he says,
pulling me close.
*At last.*

# THE CABIN

looks like
a shack with
a pull-out couch,
hot plate,
and patchwork quilt.


Sounds like
deep quiet and
rain pattering
on a tin roof.


Smells like old
cigarette tar
and bacon grease.


Tastes like
warm beer
and Cole's
cinnamon gum.


Feels like
a shiver in
the heat,

so right
and so wrong.

# THE COUCH BED

creaks like a
hundred rusty springs.

Cole lies next to me
and kisses my forehead.

Looks at me
in that way
that tells me
I'm seen.

Cole tells me I'm
beautiful.

I'm extraordinary.

I'm his angel
sent from heaven.

He knows he
doesn't deserve me.

I'm his soul mate.

The one he has
been looking for.

His eyes are
a clear blue.

This is the Cole
I know.

This is the Cole
I love.

# ARE YOU READY?

Cole asks.

I shiver.

*Um.*

# SMART GIRLS

make decisions using
pro/con lists.

I haven't made one
all summer.

But I feel myself
writing one now.

Pros of sleeping with Cole:
He will keep loving me.
We will be connected forever.
He will stay.
We can be happy.
This could be my one
shot at love.

          Cons of sleeping with Cole:
          I don't think I'm ready.
          If something goes wrong,
          that is, if something breaks,
          I could get pregnant.
          If I get pregnant,
          I can't go to college.
          I promised my Mom.
          I promised *myself.*

# SUDDENLY

I hear my mom say,

*The women in this*

*family have a*

 *w e a k n e s s*

*for bad boys.*

Suddenly,

I hear my mom say,

*From the start*

*your dad*

*was a very bad*

*idea.*

Suddenly,

I hear my mom say,

*Don't give your*

*dreams away*

*for any man,*

*Skyla-Ann.*

And suddenly,

I want my mom.

# I PUSH THE WEIGHT OF HIM

off of me
and scramble
to my feet.


My face is hot
and wet with
tears.


I can't breathe.
I can't breathe.
I can't breathe.

# COLE LOOKS CONFUSED

He steps toward me
saying, *Sky, are you—*


*No, I'm not,*
I say.
*I'm not all right.*


*Sky, are you*
*gonna do this*
*to me again?*
Cole asks.


He is hurt.


But so am I.


He reaches for me, roughly.
I pull away just as hard.


*Cole,*
I say.
I shake my head.
*I'm saying no.*

# IN A PERFECT WORLD

Cole would say,
*It's okay.*

Cole would say,
*I understand.*

Cole would say,
*Take all the time
you need.*

Cole would say,
*I love you
for you.*

Cole would say,
*Let me take
you home.*

# IN THIS CABIN

Cole says,
*I can't
believe this.*


Cole says,
*You promised.*


Cole says,
*You must not
really love me.*


Cole says,
*Get out of here.*


Cole says,
*Find your own
way home.*

# AND THAT'S HOW

I end up walking
down Route 20
in the dark.


My eyes blurry,
my nose raw.
I cry and
I cry and
I cry.


That's how
I end up with
cars whizzing
by me.


Headlights blinding.
Horns beeping.


They disappear
into the black.
And I think maybe,
just maybe,
if I keep walking
I will disappear
too.

# I CALL LAYLA

but she doesn't
answer.

She is probably
screening her calls.
I've ditched her
all summer.

> (Why would she want
> to talk to me?)

I call Zayn.

But he doesn't
answer.

He is probably
getting sleep before
the big road trip.
He is dreaming of smart girls
who walk Brooklea's
green-grass campus
every day.

> (Why would he want
> to talk to me?)

I call my mom.

But she doesn't
answer.

She is probably
on the couch with
Darron, in the
spot where I used to
fit.

(What would I even
say?)

I hang up
instead of leaving
a voicemail,
and that's when—

# IT HITS ME

White light.

No sound.

Going

going

gone.

(Bad idea,

Sky.

Bad.

Idea.)

# I AM EIGHT YEARS OLD

Mom is sick.
> *Just a cold*, she says.


She coughs all night.
She is hot under my fingertips.
She is gray and shivering.


At some point,
our neighbor
takes her
to the hospital.


I sit next to Mom
even when the nurses
try to make me leave.


We watch TV
and I read her chapter books
and she gives me a dinner roll
to eat from her tray.


I remember her doctor
dressed in white, all
white. She had this voice,
and I can hear it now—

# HEAVEN

*Skyler*,

the voice says.


But I am deep

inside a web,

all twisted

and tangled

in white.


Skyler Wise,

the ultimate prize

all

dressed

in

white.

# AND THEN PAIN

So much pain
       that I have to
              take an inventory.


My head feels
       as if it's
              been carved
                     like a pumpkin.


My legs feel
       as if they are
              full of gravel.


My arms feel
       as if someone is
              dabbing cuts
                     with vinegar.


My chest feels
       tight, like
              I might never
                     catch my breath.

# AWAKE

*She's awake.*

A new voice.

Familiar.

Whose?

Zayn.

# IN THE MOVIES

when someone wakes up,
they bat their eyes
      oh so *softly*.


But my eyes are
crusty from crying
      oh so *badly*.


And the first sight
I see is my Mom
      oh so *sad*.


And then Layla
standing by,
      not so *mad*.


And Zayn holding
my hand,
      oh so *tight*.


For just a moment
things feel
      oh so *right*.

# MY HEART POUNDS

the moment I sit up
o
u
c
h
And my mom smoothes my hair.
s
i
g
h
She says I gave her quite a scare.
w
h
y
?
She says I could have died.
w
o
a
h

# A COP COMES

She wants to know *why*
I was walking on a
country road in the
middle of the night
alone.

She wants to know *what*
I was doing so far
from home when that car
hit me so hard.

She wants to know *when*
I left home and what
happened between then
and the accident.

She wants to know *where*
I came from and
where I was trying
to go.

She wants to know *who*
I was with that night.
Who left me
for dead.

# WHO?

*Him.*

*Him who?*

*I need to talk to him.*

*Skyler, what's his name?*

*Name like fire.*
*Cole Baker.*

# NEVER

*You are never speaking*
*to that boy again,*
my mom says
when the cop leaves.


Layla bites her lip.


Zayn stands in a corner
picking under his nails.
He doesn't look
at me.


*Mom, I need to tell him that—*


*That you could have died?*
she asks.


*That I'm alive,*
I say.

# I'M NOT SURE

if it's because
I saw the white light
and almost walked
toward it.


Or if it's because
I'm addicted
to the sound of
his voice.


Or if it's because
I don't feel myself
when he's not here
to tell me
who I am.


But my hands are
shaky. My lips
tremble with the
need to talk
to him.


I
need
him
now.

# GET OUT

I say to my mom
and Layla
and Zayn.

> *Get out*
> *if you're going*
> *to judge me.*

> *God, I'm not perfect.*

> *Can't you see?*

> *Get out if you don't*
> *love me for me.*

It might be the hospital painkillers.
It might be Cole's words
in my head.

But mostly        it's me
breaking          apart
at the            seams.

# HIS PHONE RINGS

On the first ring, I imagine
      myself saying,
      *You have to know*
      *I love you.*

On the second ring, I imagine
      myself saying,
      *I shouldn't have left.*

On the third ring, I imagine
      myself saying,
      *I could have died*
      *that night.*

On the fourth ring, I imagine
      myself saying,
      *Don't you even care*
      *about me?*

When it goes to voicemail,
I get the message.

# AN EQUATION

7 days in the ICU

+

10 days in a hospital room

+

2 weeks bed rest at home

=

The worst end to a summer.

Ever.

# RELATIONSHIPS HEAL

like broken bones—
slowly and sometimes
painfully.


I don't speak to Mom
for two whole days.
She never leaves
my side, not even when
the nurses try to kick
her out at night.


Then one day,
I wake up to feel her
cheek on my forehead.
Checking for a fever.
And in that moment,
I feel so *felt*.

# MOM SAYS IT FIRST

*I'm sorry, baby girl.*
*I know I need to*
*let you fly.*
*I know I need to*
*keep an open mind.*
*I know I need to*
*let you make*
*your own mistakes.*

*I'm sorry, Mama.*
*I know I need to*
*be more honest.*
*I know I need to*
*be more careful.*
*I know that I need*
*you now more than*
*ever.*

# LAYLA ANSWERS

on the
first ring.

*I am so sorry,*
I say.

*Oh, Wise One,*
she says,
*I'm coming over.*

## YOU MADE IT

Mom says.
Seventeen.
Older than she was
when she got pregnant
with me.


I think I will
spend the whole day
bored at the hospital.
But then Layla
pops her head in.
Followed by Zayn.
Followed by a cake.


And they get permission
to wheel me out to
a common area
to sing "Happy Birthday."


*Make a wish*,
Zayn says and we
            lock eyes
before I blow out
the candles.

*What did you wish for?*
*What do you want?*
Layla asks.


It's the same question
          Cole Baker
asked me months ago.

# WHAT I WANT

Months ago,
I was open to suggestion.
Months ago,
I didn't have my own answer.
Months ago,
I didn't have my own voice.


But now I say, clearly,
to everyone
in that room,


*I want to go to college.*
     (And I mean it.)
*I want to play music.*
      (And I mean that, too.)
*Maybe I even want*
*to go to school for music.*
     (That last part
     I don't mean.
     I know I want to be
     a doctor but want to
     see how Mom reacts.
     She nods—it's okay.)


*May all your wishes*
*come true, baby girl,*
Mom says.

182

# HAPPY BIRTHDAY

Those two words
spoken out loud
by the ones I love
are a gift.


Those two words
texted to me
by the boy I used to love
feel like a curse.


A choice: to text back
and lose myself again
or put my phone down
and eat my cake.


And this time,
I choose to eat cake.

# LAYLA SAYS

*You don't need to*
*give it all*
*to the*
*first person*
*who buys*
*you tacos*
*and calls*
*you*
*beautiful.*

Today,
I think she
might be
the wise one.

# TOO LATE

Two weeks too late,
Cole calls me 15 times.
Cole leaves five long messages.
Cole texts me every night.


Cole says he loves me. Will die
without me. But I know now that
love is more than racing hearts and
long kisses and crazy adventures.


Love is keeping someone
safe. Respecting each
*no*. And letting them spread
their wings to fly.

# SOME THINGS HAVEN'T CHANGED

Layla and Zayn sit on my couch
until summer ends and
watch terrible '80s movies
        and make terrible jokes.


Layla tells me all about
        the new girl
she's seeing and how she
        seems to fit just right.


Zayn makes me apple pancakes.
        He makes me laugh
so hard I can feel my healing
        ribs crackle.


And even though my heart
        feels as broken as my bones,
it still feels so full of the things
        I almost lost.

# MOM'S SECRET

Turns out,
>Mom had another secret.
>One she never wanted
>to have to tell me.


Turns out,
>Mom knows what I'm
>going through as I try
>to detox from Cole.


Turns out,
>Mom was hurt
>by my dad in more ways
>than just his leaving.


Turns out,
>my dad was more than
>just a bad idea. He was
>a bad idea with a temper,
>despite his charm.


Turns out,
>Mom made him leave
>so he couldn't hurt me ever.
>And she promised herself
>no man ever would.

# THE WOMEN IN THIS FAMILY

used to have a

       w e a k n e s s

for bad boys.

But now my mom is
       with Darron.

He sings sappy love songs
out of key.
He wears too-big sweaters.
He wouldn't hurt us, ever.
And Mom loves him.

And now I am sitting
       with Zayn.

He's teaching me a
card game. His long hair
falls in his face. And I
suddenly see him, like
for the first time.

And I think:
Maybe we've broken the curse
of the women in this family.

# THE ROAD IN FRONT OF ME

is even more beautiful
in late fall
than in summer.


I am nearly healed now,
heart and bone.
Zayn takes the back
roads to Brooklea
and I sit shotgun.


He turns up the music,
a mix he made, of all
my favorite songs.
I sing along,
and he listens.

## STOP

I have just one last

        little

                bad

                        idea.

I see a sign and say,

        *Please*

                *stop*

                        *here.*

Zayn parks the car right

        on

                the

                        sand.

And I know what I

        have

                to

                        do.

# ONE STEP AT A TIME

I walk toward the freezing surf.
   I leave my crutches behind.
Icy water soaks my cast.


I walk in, until the water
   touches the edge of my dress.
My fingertips make ripples.


And in that moment, my whole life
   is laid ahead of me.
All the good ideas and bad ideas.


All of my victories and all of
   my mistakes and heartbreaks.
There will be more of each.


In that moment,
   I am unbreakable,
untouchable, awake, and alive.


In that moment,
   I am totally free,
my eyes on endless sky.

# WANT TO KEEP READING?

If you liked this book, check out another book
from West 44 Books:

## *THE SAME BLOOD* BY M. AZMITIA

ISBN: 9781538382516

You have foggy memories
of Puerto Rico. Hazy.

Like a dream you can
never quite grasp come
morning.

You remember
being six years old. Stepping

barefoot

into an orange-
tiled fountain
with Mel.

     Finding your shoes in
     grass overrun with ants.

You remember
a beach,

deserted

and covered in
seaweed.

Green waves
that knocked you back
onto the shore.

Mel laughing as
she helped you
stand—
    *You okay, Elena?*

        The way you sulked
        because it wasn't safe
        for you to swim.

When a volcano's
ash keeps you from

        flying home,

you cry and tell Mami
you miss your dog.

# ABOUT THE AUTHOR

Caitie McKay is a writer and children's book editor from Buffalo, New York. She graduated with a degree in creative writing from Canisius College, where she was awarded the G.E. Murray Award for Excellence in Creative Writing. She's written and edited more than 500 educational books for children. This is her first novel. For more information, visit caitiemcwritesalot.com.

THE
Blood
M. AZMITIA

ONE
too many
LIES
L.A. BOWEN

Dreams on
FIRE
Annette Daniels Taylor

CASA DE PIZZA

FIFTEEN
AND
CHANGE
MAX HOWARD

Check out more books at:
www.west44books.com